10/15

In life there are sore losers,
and there are sore winners.

Zeke Meeks is published by
Picture Window Books,
A Capstone Imprint
1710 Roe Crest Drive
North Mankato, Minnesota 56003
www.capstonepub.com

Library of Congress Cataloging-in-Publication Data
Green, D. L. (Debra L.), author.
  Zeke Meeks vs the stinky soccer team / by D. L. Green; illustrated by Josh Alves.
      pages cm. — (Zeke Meeks)
Summary: Third-grader Zeke's soccer experience is proving to be a disaster — all of his
friends are on a different team, while his team is dominated by a bully who hogs the ball
and knocks down anyone who gets in his way.
ISBN 978-1-4795-5768-4 (hardcover)
ISBN 978-1-4795-5770-7 (paperback)
ISBN 978-1-4795-6210-7 (eBook)
1. Soccer stories. 2. Middle-born children—Juvenile fiction. 3. Brothers and sisters—Juvenile
fiction. 4. Bullying—Juvenile fiction. 5. Teamwork (Sports)—Juvenile fiction. [1. Soccer—
Fiction. 2. Humorous stories.] I. Alves, Josh, illustrator. II. Title. III. Title: Zeke Meeks
versus the stinky soccer team. IV. Series: Green, D. L. (Debra L.) Zeke Meeks.
  PZ7.G81926Zif 2015
  813.6—dc23   2014022381

Vector Credits: Shutterstock
Book design by: Kristi Carlson

Printed in China.
092014   008472RRDS15

Worst. Kid. EVER.
You think Grace Chang
is bad? Wait until you
meet Bolt. Yes. His
name is BOLT.

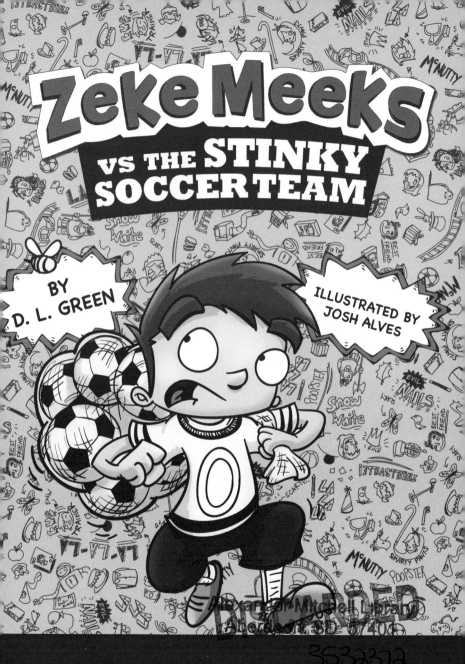

Zeke Meeks
vs the STINKY SOCCER TEAM

BY
D. L. GREEN

ILLUSTRATED BY
JOSH ALVES

PICTURE WINDOW BOOKS
a capstone imprint

The best thing about soccer? The snacks.

TABLE OF

Guess who is the Moronic Moron and who is the Ball Hog?

A ball hog. Get it?

EVERYTHING BUT THE PLAYGROUND

BOYS RULE

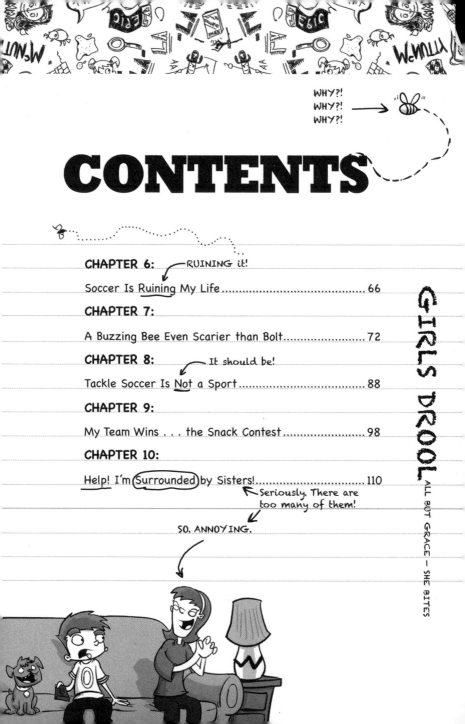

WHY?!
WHY?!
WHY?!

CONTENTS

⸺Seriously. There are too many of them!

SO, ANNOYING.

GIRLS DROOL ALL BUT GRACE — SHE BITES

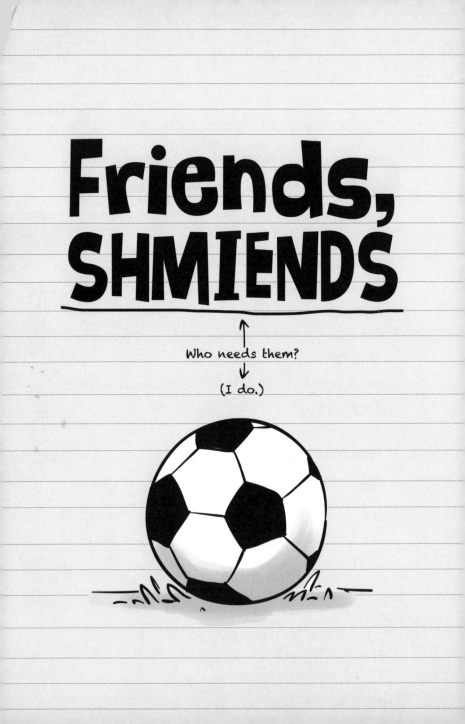

My mom drove me to my first soccer team meeting. As she drove, she talked. And talked. And talked.

I didn't listen. Instead, I gazed out the car window and imagined my first soccer game. I'd wear a very cool red or black jersey. I'd score at least five goals. My teammates would shout, "Go, Zeke! Go, Zeke! Go, Zeke!"

We'd win the game. We'd win all of our games. Then we'd get huge gold trophies.

Mom stopped at a red light. She asked, "Were you listening to me, Zeke? Did you hear one single word I just said?"

I nodded. "I heard every single word you just said. You said, 'Were you listening to me, Zeke? Did you hear one single word I just said?'"

BUT DID YOU HEAR ANYTHING I SAID BEFORE THAT?

Mom drove into the parking lot of the soccer field. I nodded again. "Yes, I heard what you said before."

My ears had heard everything she'd said, but my brain hadn't paid attention. My brain was filled with a ton of my own thoughts. It had no room for my mother's thoughts.

As my mom looked for a parking spot, I looked for my friends from school. Hector Cruz, Owen Leach, and Rudy Morse had all said they had a soccer team meeting today. It was going to be fun to play on a team with them. Where were they?

Mom parked the car and said, "As I told you in the car, playing soccer will teach you to be a good sport."

"I'll be a good sport. I won't brag too much after my team wins every game," I replied.

"You might not win every game. You might not even win any game. But that's not important," Mom said.

"Of course it's important. It's very important. Winning is the most important thing," I explained to my mother.

She shook her head. "Exercise is more important. Soccer will make your body stronger."

I rolled my eyes. "Exercise, shmexercise. Stronger, shmonger."

"It's also important to learn teamwork," Mom said.

"Teamwork, shmeamwork. Winning is what really counts," I said. My mother was smart about some things but not about soccer. She didn't understand soccer at all.

I got out of the car and looked for my friends. I still didn't see anyone I knew.

Something flew in front of me. It was not a friend. It was an enemy. It was terrifying. It was a flea!

My mouth dropped open. I hoped the flea wouldn't fly into it. I wanted to close my mouth, but I was frozen with fear.

Mom got out of the car. She pointed to the horrifying bug in front of me and said, "Look at that itsy bitsy, teensy weensy, tiny little flea. It's so cute."

I didn't think it was cute. Not at all. Bugs scared me. Even tiny ones like fleas terrified me. I didn't tell people that. It was embarrassing. I didn't even tell my mom.

Suddenly Mom did something very brave: She waved her hand in front of the flea.

The flea flew away, ready to terrorize other people. Or maybe just pester them a little.

I was finally able to close my mouth. And I did.

Mom pointed to a man on the soccer field. He held a sign that said, "Coach Hall's Soccer Team." A lot of boys and parents stood around him. I didn't see my friends there or anyone else I knew.

"That's your soccer team," Mom said.

I frowned. I was supposed to be on a team with my friends. Where were they?

TINKLE, TINKLE, Little Star

Certain colors should only be found in toilets.

Mom and I walked over to Coach Hall and my new teammates.

A short kid smiled at me and said, "Hi. I'm Raj Patel. I'm in third grade at Granada Academy."

I smiled back. "I'm Zeke Meeks. I'm in third grade at Worthsome Elementary School."

A tall boy frowned at us and said, "I don't care what grade you're in or where you go to school. The only thing that matters is whether or not you're a good soccer player. My name is Bolt Burley. I'm a great soccer player."

A tall woman said, "I'm Bolt's mother. Bolt really is a great soccer player."

"Nice to meet you," I said. I looked around. I didn't know any of the boys there.

My mom put her hand on my shoulder. "What's wrong, Zeke? You seem upset."

"I don't know a single person here. Where are my friends?" I asked.

"I don't know. But being on a soccer team is a terrific way to make new friends. Now you've met Raj and Bolt. You'll get to know them better soon," Mom said.

I kicked the grass. I didn't want to make new friends. I wanted to be with my old friends.

Coach Hall held up a pair of black shorts in one hand. In the other hand, he held up a soccer jersey and soccer socks. They were the color of pee. He said, "Here is our team uniform."

I groaned.

A few other kids groaned, too.

"It doesn't matter what our uniforms look like," Bolt said.

Mom nodded. "That boy has a good attitude. It doesn't matter what you look like. More important is what's on the inside: character, kindness, and spirit."

"The only thing that matters is winning," Bolt said. "We have to win, win, win. If we don't win all our games, I'll be furious." He pumped his fist and growled.

Mom shook her head. "Never mind. That boy doesn't have a good attitude."

"We need to choose a name for our team," the coach said.

"We'll call ourselves the Buzzing Bees," Bolt said. "Bees are yellow and black, like our yellow jerseys and black shorts."

Bees! No! I did not want to think about scary insects every time I wore my soccer uniform. Bees were even scarier than fleas. They loudly buzzed and painfully stung.

I tried to think of another name that went along with our pee-colored jerseys. Aha! I thought of one. I said, "We could call ourselves Team Urine."

"Or the Tinklers," Raj said.

"Or Team Pee Pee," a boy said.

Coach Hall shook his head. "You can't name yourself after pee pee."

"How about the Stinging Wasps? Wasps are yellow and black," another boy suggested.

"No!" I exclaimed. Stinging wasps were even scarier than buzzing bees.

"My idea is the best. Our team should be the Buzzing Bees," Bolt said.

"Wait," I said. I tried to think of other yellow things to use for a team name.

"Hurry up," Bolt ordered.

"Um, um, um . . . How about the Lemons?" I said.

"That's an awful name," Bolt said.

"The Honeys?" I knew the Honeys wasn't a great name, but I had to try.

"That's the name of my sister's team. And she's in kindergarten," Bolt said.

"The Daisies?" I suggested.

Bolt scowled. "That's a little girl name, too. We'll call our team the Buzzing Bees."

"Okay," a boy said.

"Fine," another boy said.

"Good enough," another boy said.

"All right. Our team name is the Buzzing Bees," Coach Hall said. I sighed.

The coach gave each of us a uniform.

"My jersey has a nine on it. So I'm number nine. That's perfect, because I'm nine years old," a boy said.

"I'm number seven. It's my lucky number," Raj said.

"I got number zero." I sighed again. There was nothing good about being a zero.

Bolt held up his uniform. "I'm number one. That's perfect for me, because I'm the number-one soccer player."

He was the number-one bossy bragger. I didn't like Bolt. I also didn't like having no friends on the team. And I didn't like our pee-colored uniforms. I really didn't like our scary Buzzing Bees team name.

In conclusion, I didn't like a single thing about my new soccer team.

"Hello," a woman said. "I'm in charge of snacks for the team. Parents will take turns bringing snacks at every game. Today I brought cupcakes." She gave each boy a giant chocolate cupcake covered with thick, fluffy mounds of vanilla frosting and a ton of colorful sprinkles.

Okay, I liked one thing about my new soccer team: the snacks.

PRINCESS SING-ALONG: The ONLY Girl WORSE than My Sisters

The only thing worse than Princess Sing-Along is bugs. And Bolt.

When I got home from the soccer team
meeting, I sniffed my new uniform. "At least it
doesn't smell like pee," I said.

"Of course it doesn't smell like pee. It doesn't
look like pee either. It's a nice yellow color, like
a sweet honeybee or a pretty wasp," Mom said.

She was wrong. My uniform looked like pee.
And there was nothing nice, sweet, or pretty
about bees or wasps.

My little sister, Mia, came into the living room. As soon as she spotted my soccer shirt, she frowned.

"What's wrong?" I asked.

"I told you so," I said to Mom.

Mom shook her head. "It does not look like pee."

"It really does," said my older sister, Alexa.

"That reminds me of a Princess Sing-Along song," Mia said.

"Please don't sing any Princess Sing-Along songs," I said. Princess Sing-Along was the star of a terrible TV show for little kids. She sang awful songs in a screechy voice. Mia loved the show.

"Don't worry," Mia said. "I won't sing just any Princess Sing-Along song. I'll sing a very special one." Before I could stop her, Mia screeched, "Before a long car ride, la la la, make sure that you have tried, la la la, to go tinkle in the potty, la la la. So you won't pee on your body, la la la."

"Gross," I said.

"Zeke, I remember when you were Mia's age. One day you fell asleep in the car and peed in your pants," Alexa said.

"Gross," Mia said.

I crossed my arms. "Leave me alone."

"Zeke is in a bad mood," Mom said.

"If my soccer shirt looked like pee pee, I'd be in a bad mood too," Mia said.

"Cheer up, Zeke. At least your soccer shirt isn't the color of poop," Alexa said.

"Or the color of throw up," Mia added.

"Or snot," Alexa said.

I did not cheer up.

"I'm glad I don't have to wear a soccer shirt that looks like pee. I don't have to wear any soccer shirts, because I don't play soccer. I play the sport of jump rope," Mia said.

I didn't think jump rope was really a sport. But I didn't tell Mia that. If she was busy jumping rope, she wouldn't have time for Princess Sing-Along songs. I told her, "You should do the sport of jump rope now."

"Good idea." Mia got her jump rope from her bedroom.

Then she sang an annoying Princess Sing-Along song: "Brush your teeth twice a day, la la la. So they won't rot away, la la la.

"I thought you were going to jump rope," I said.

"I am," she replied. "While I'm jumping rope, I always sing Princess Sing-Along songs."

I groaned.

Mia sang, "It is very rude to groan, la la la. It's also rude to sigh and moan, la la la."

I went to my bedroom and closed the door behind me. Then I groaned, sighed, and moaned.

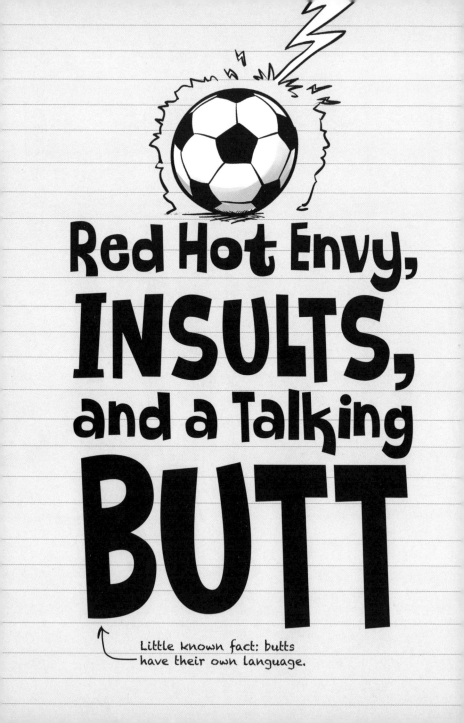

Red Hot Envy, INSULTS, and a Talking BUTT

Little known fact: butts have their own language.

Once I got to school the next morning, I ran to the playground to find my friends.

Hector and Owen were kicking around a soccer ball. I told them, "I didn't see you guys at the soccer team meeting yesterday."

"We were there," Hector said. He kicked the ball to Owen.

"Rudy went to the meeting too," Owen said. He kicked the ball back to Hector.

"You were on the soccer field yesterday at four o'clock?" I asked.

Hector nodded. "At the North Cheeseham field with Coach Ming."

I frowned. "I was at the South Cheeseham field with Coach Hall. We must be on different teams."

"Too bad. Who's on your team?" Hector asked.

"I don't know anyone on my team," I said. I thought about bossy bragger Bolt and added, "And I don't want to know anyone on my team."

"Hector, Rudy, and I are all on the Red Hot Lightning. That's our team name," Owen said.

Red Hot Lightning was a cool name. It was a thousand times better than the Buzzing Bees.

"When we run fast in our awesome red soccer uniforms, it looks like we're on fire," Hector said.

"You get to wear red uniforms?" I asked.

Hector nodded.

They were so lucky. Red was one of my favorite colors.

Hector dribbled the ball from one foot to the other. He asked, "What's your team name, Zeke?"

"I bet it's not as cool as Red Hot Lightning," Owen said.

"Don't be mean. I'm sure Zeke's team name is cool," Hector said.

I sighed. "My team is called the Buzzing Bees."

"I told you it wasn't cool," Owen said.

"Does your team have cool uniforms?"
Hector asked me.

I pictured our soccer jerseys. They would be
cool if urine was cool. But urine was definitely
not cool.

I didn't answer Hector's question about our uniforms. Instead, I said, "We'd better get to class."

"But we still have a few minutes before school starts," Hector said.

I didn't want to spend any of those few minutes talking about my team's urine uniforms. I waved goodbye to my friends and walked to the classroom.

My teacher, Mr. McNutty, looked up from his desk.

ZEKE, WHAT'S WRONG?

"Nothing," I replied, even though a lot was wrong.

"You usually come into my classroom half a second before the bell rings. Why are you here so early today?" Mr. McNutty asked.

"I'm eager to learn," I said.

"You? Eager to learn?" Mr. McNutty laughed. "Why are you really here so early?"

Victoria Crow walked into the room and said, "I'm eager to learn."

I believed that. Victoria was the smartest kid in third grade.

"I'm the smartest kid in third grade," Victoria said.

I nodded. "I know. You tell everyone that all the time."

"That's because I don't know whether other people are smart enough to remember what I tell them," she said.

"If you were smarter, you'd know whether other people were smart enough to remember what you tell them," I said.

"Huh? Is that an insult?" she asked me.

"If you were smarter, you'd know if that was an insult," I said.

Victoria glared at me. "That's definitely an insult."

"Stop arguing, kids," Mr. McNutty said.

"All right, Mr. McNutty. I'd much rather learn things than argue with people who aren't as smart as me," Victoria said.

I would much rather argue with people than learn things. I'd rather do almost anything than learn things. But I was smart enough not to tell Mr. McNutty that.

The rest of the class started coming into the room.

"Oh, good. School is about to begin. I hope we get to do hard math problems, read long books, and fill out tough science worksheets today," Victoria said.

"I hope we get to watch movies, draw simple things, and do P.E. today," I said.

Half a second before the bell rang, Hector and Owen rushed into class and hurried to their desks.

"We have challenging work today," said Mr. McNutty.

"Hurray!" Victoria said. "I love challenges. It's hard to challenge me. That's because I'm the smartest kid in third grade."

She was also the most boastful kid in third grade.

Mr. McNutty said, "We will start with —"

"A movie?" I asked.

"No," he said.

"Drawing simple pictures?" I asked.

"No," he said.

"P.E.?"

"Please stop talking. I get distracted by interruptions," he said.

That was my plan. I wanted to distract him from giving us challenging work.

"I don't want to hear any more talking," Mr. McNutty said.

Rudy let out a loud fart.

"I told you not to interrupt me," said Mr. McNutty.

"You said not to talk. You didn't say anything about farting," Rudy said.

"Rudy, your butt talked," I said.

The class laughed.

"The next person who interrupts me will stay inside during lunch," Mr. McNutty said.

I wondered whether I should interrupt him again. Staying inside might be a good idea.

If I stayed inside during lunch, I wouldn't have to hear about my friends' terrific soccer team or answer questions about my terrible team. I didn't want anyone at school to find out about my pee-colored uniform.

"If you stay inside during lunch, you'll have to clean the classroom," Mr. McNutty said.

I didn't like sitting inside all day. I really didn't like cleaning the classroom. So I didn't interrupt Mr. McNutty again.

But I did pass a note to Victoria that said:

She sent the note back to me. She'd corrected my mistakes with a red pen:

I sighed and put my head on my desk.

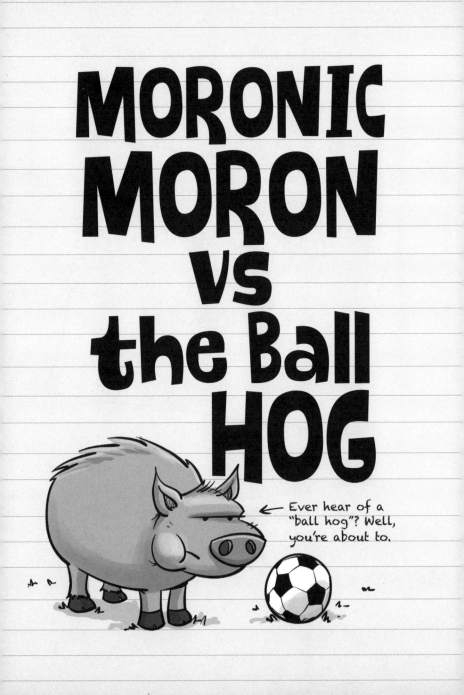

On Saturday, we huddled around Coach Hall on the sideline of the soccer field. Our families stood behind us. "Our first game starts in a few minutes. Everyone try your best and have fun," the coach said.

"And win. Win, win, win," Bolt said.

"Win, win, win," his mother repeated.

"Winning is nice," the coach said.

"Winning isn't just nice. It's extremely important," Bolt said.

"And extremely necessary," Bolt's mother added.

"It's more important to learn new skills, exercise, make friends, practice good —"

Bolt cut him off. "We need to win. Win, win, win."

"Win, win, win," Bolt's mother chanted.

"Our soccer games are just for fun. We don't even keep score," the coach said.

"I'll keep score. If we don't win, I'll be very angry." Bolt made a fist.

"Me too." Bolt's mother made a fist.

Bolt pumped his fist in the air.

His mother pumped her fist in the air too.

My annoying sister Mia sang an annoying Princess Sing-Along song: "Nobody wins every game, la la la. So a loss shouldn't bring you shame, la la la. You shouldn't whine or cry or scream, la la la, if you're on a stinky team, la la la."

"I won't cry if we don't win," Bolt said.

"That's good sportsmanship," the coach said.

"But I will scream. And punch people. And possibly kick people too," Bolt said.

"That's bad sportsmanship," the coach said.

Mia nodded. "Yeah. Princess Sing-Along says —"

Bolt cut her off. "Be quiet. You're annoying. And so are your songs."

Mia stuck out her lower lip and blinked her eyes a bunch of times. It looked like she was trying not to cry.

Mia and her songs were annoying, but I didn't like people telling her that. Okay, *I* told her that. But I didn't like it when *other* people told her that. Especially when those other people were mean kids like Bolt. I said, "Bolt. You upset my sister. Leave her —"

The referee blew his whistle. That signaled the teams to get on the field to start the game.

I was glad the whistle interrupted me. I didn't want Bolt to scream at me or punch me or kick me or do all three.

We got on the field and faced the Gold Storm team. Their gold uniforms looked kind of like our yellow uniforms, except they weren't the color of pee.

I played in the midfield. Midfield players tried to score goals and get the ball away from the other team. Midfielders had to run all over the soccer field. It was very tiring.

Bolt got the ball and kicked it to me. I caught the ball with my foot and dribbled it down the field. I ran super fast.

My teammates shouted at me. I couldn't hear what they said, but they sounded very excited. Having them cheer for me felt great. It made me run faster.

The Gold Storm's defense was awful. They didn't block me at all, even when I got close to the goal.

I kicked the ball into the goal and scored the first point of the game.

I loved soccer! And I was so good at it! Maybe I would become a pro soccer player and have millions of fans and make millions of dollars. I waved my arms in the air and shouted, "Hooray!"

The Gold Storm players also waved their arms in the air and shouted, "Hooray!" It was nice of them to root for me. They sure were good sports.

Then Bolt shouted, "Zeke Meeks, you moronic moron! You scored a goal for the other team."

I did? I looked around me. Uh-oh. I was standing in front of our goalie. The Gold Storm players were still cheering. But most of the Buzzing Bees players were groaning.

"What a moron!" Bolt screamed. He punched and kicked the air.

"It's all right, Zeke. Everyone makes mistakes," Raj said.

"It isn't all right. Only a moronic moron makes mistakes!" Bolt shouted.

Mom called out, "It's okay, honey. Good try."

Bolt's mom shouted, "It's not okay. Bad try!"

Bolt kept punching and kicking the air.

At least he didn't punch and kick me.

The referee blew his whistle. He pointed at Bolt and said, "Stop acting like a bad sport, or I'll give you a penalty."

"You should give Zeke Meeks a penalty for playing so terribly," Bolt's mom said.

"Parents shouldn't act like bad sports either," the referee said.

We lined up on the field again. Bolt said, "Listen, everyone. Don't let Zeke get the ball. He might score more goals for the other team. I'll keep the ball from now on."

Bolt dribbled the soccer ball up the field.

Coach Hall yelled, "Bolt, pass the ball to someone near the goal!"

Bolt ignored the coach. He tried to kick the ball into the goal but missed. He was too far away.

The Gold Storm got the ball and passed it back and forth to each other, all the way down the field. Then the player closest to the goal kicked it in. The team cheered again.

A Gold Storm player near me said, "The score is two to zero. We're winning. You're losing. Ha-ha."

"We're not supposed to keep score," I said.

"It's two to zero and everyone knows it." He stuck out his tongue.

"Just try your best, Zeke," Mom said.

"Try your best not to play like awful little babies!" Bolt's mother yelled.

I tried my best for a few more minutes. Then I stopped trying my best.

It was useless, because I never got the ball. Bolt kept hogging it. He wouldn't pass it to me or anyone else.

Bolt made two goals in the game, but the Gold Storm team made many more. The final score was eight to two.

After the game, Coach Hall held another meeting. Everyone on my team was frowning. A couple of kids were kicking the dirt. Our coach said, "The score doesn't matter. No one keeps track."

"I kept track of the score. It was two to eight," Bolt said.

"I kept track too. It was two to eight," another kid said.

"Yep. Two to eight," another kid said.

"Bolt, you need to pass the ball to your teammates," Coach Hall said.

Bolt shook his head. "I tried that, but Zeke Meeks made a goal for the Gold Storm."

"This is a team sport. Play with the team. Soccer should be fun for everyone," our coach said.

It wasn't fun for me. I had embarrassed myself by scoring for the Gold Storm. I'd been yelled at by Bolt and his mom. And our team had lost. There was nothing fun about playing soccer.

"After all that healthy exercise, you Buzzing Bees deserve a snack," Raj's mother said.

She gave each Buzzing Bee a giant slice of chocolate cake with chocolate frosting.

Okay, there was one fun thing about playing soccer: the snacks.

But even delicious chocolate cake couldn't make up for the horrible game.

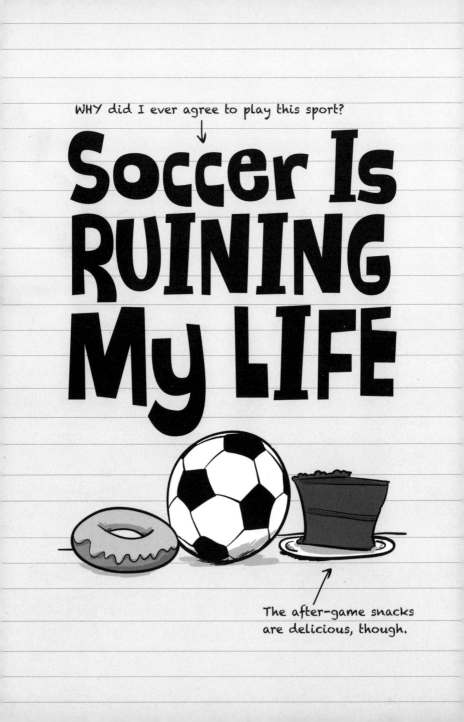

Once Mom dropped me off at school on Monday morning, I joined my friends on the playground. Hector, Owen, and Rudy were kicking around a soccer ball.

"How was your game, Zeke?" Owen asked.

I shrugged. I didn't want to admit that my team had lost. I really didn't want to admit that I'd scored a goal for the other team. But I also didn't want to lie. So I changed the subject. "How was your game, Owen?"

"I scored three goals," he said as he dribbled the soccer ball.

"Three goals is great," I said.

"Scoring three goals is awesome. Our team is awesome too. We won our game. The score was seven to four," Rudy said.

"We got to eat big glazed donuts after the game." Hector licked his lips.

"Zeke, you didn't answer my question. How was your game?" Owen asked.

"I made a goal. The final score was eight to two. We got to eat huge slices of chocolate cake," I said. I had told the truth. Sort of. I really did make a goal — for the other team. And the score was eight to two — for the other team. We truly did get huge slices of chocolate cake.

"I love soccer," Rudy said.

I nodded. "I agree." I agreed that Rudy loved soccer.

"We have a great team," Owen said.

"My team is great too," I said. We were great at yelling and losing.

"I love getting snacks after the games," Hector said.

"Me too," I said completely truthfully.

"We'll find out soon how great Zeke's team is." Owen kicked the ball to me.

I missed the ball and had to chase it across the playground. When I returned to my friends, I asked, "How will you find out how great my team is?"

"On Saturday, our great team plays your great team," Owen said.

"Oh," I said.

Oh, no. On Saturday, my friends would find out I'd lied to them. They'd find out that my team wasn't great or even good.

My friends would find out that my team was very bad.

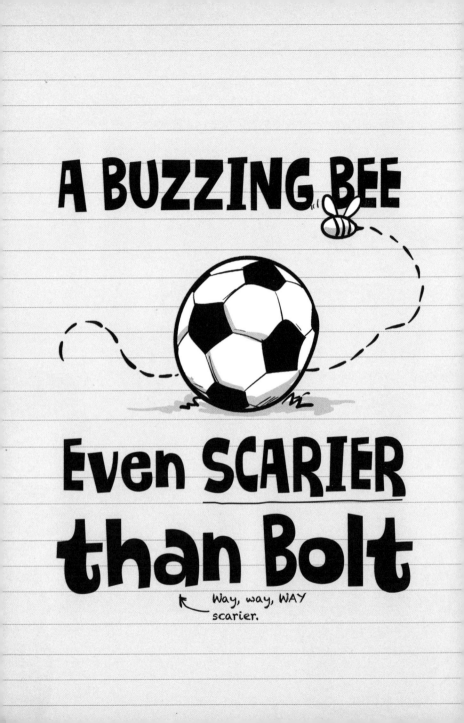

Mom walked into my bedroom on Saturday morning. She said, "You need to get ready. You're playing soccer today."

There were many reasons why I did not want to play soccer:

1. My horrible team was going to play my friends' great team.

2. My horrible team was going to lose.

3. My friends would find out I'd lied about being on a great team.

4. Bolt and his mother would scream at everyone.

5. Bolt might also punch and kick people.

6. Bolt might punch and kick me.

There was only one reason to play soccer that day:

1. I'd probably get a delicious snack after the game.

Eating a delicious snack wasn't worth losing to my friends' team and getting yelled at and possibly punched and kicked.

I told my mom, "I don't want to play soccer today."

"You have to play. Your coach and your teammates are counting on you," Mom said.

I had scored a goal for the other team. My coach and teammates would probably be happy if I stopped playing soccer.

"I have a sore throat. I'm too sick to play soccer today," I said.

"You don't sound like you have a sore throat," Mom said.

Oops. I'd forgotten to act sick. I faked a cough. Then I made my voice sound raspy.

Mom shook her head. "You sound like you're faking a sore throat."

I rubbed my leg and said, "My leg hurts. I can't run on the soccer field today."

"You can sit on the sideline and watch the game with Mia and me. You need to support your team."

If I sat with my mom and little sister at the game, Bolt would probably call me a wimp or a baby or a chicken. He might even call me all three names at once. He could call me a wimpy baby chicken or a chicken baby wimp or a baby chicken wimp.

Bolt's mom might call me even worse names, like a super wimpy, weird little baby chicken butt.

"My leg feels better now," I said. "I guess I have to play soccer today. I mean, I guess I get to play soccer today."

Mom smiled. "Good."

A few minutes later, my family ate breakfast together. Mom asked my sister Alexa, "Do you want to watch Zeke play soccer today?"

"I can't watch any soccer games. I'm allergic," Alexa replied.

"Allergic to what?" I asked her.

"Boredom," she said.

"I'll entertain you with Princess Sing-Along songs," Mia said. She sang in a screechy voice, "It's fun to go to the park, la la la. But don't do it in the dark, la la la. If you cannot see your shoe, la la la, you might step in gross dog doo, la la la."

"Princess Sing-Along Songs are annoying. Being annoyed is even worse than being bored," Alexa said.

Mom, Mia and I went to the soccer field, leaving Alexa at home.

At the team meeting before the game, Coach Hall said, "Pass the ball to other players. Don't keep it to yourself." He looked right at Bolt.

"Last week, I passed the ball to another player. Then he made a goal for the other team," Bolt said. He looked right at me.

"Everyone makes mistakes," Raj said.

"I don't," Bolt said.

I rolled my eyes.

Raj rolled his eyes too.

After our team meeting, we lined up on the field across from the Red Hot Lightning team.

"Hi, Zeke!" Hector called out.

"Hey, Zeke," Owen said.

"Hello, Zeke," Rudy said.

I waved at them. "Good to see you, Hector, Owen, and Rudy."

Bolt sneered at them and said, "We'll tear your terrible team to tiny tatters."

"Calm down," Hector said.

Raj got the ball first.

"Pass it to me!" Bolt shouted.

Raj kicked the ball to Bolt.

Bolt dribbled the ball down the field, kicked it hard, and made a goal. He said, "I am an amazing soccer player."

I rolled my eyes again.

Red Hot Lightning got the ball. Hector passed it to Owen. Owen passed it to Rudy.

I tried to steal the ball.

Then I heard frightening sounds: "*Buzz, buzz, buzz.*" There were actual buzzing bees on the field.

"Buzzing bees!" I shouted in terror.

"Go Buzzing Bees!" Mom and Mia yelled. They were cheering for my team.

I was not cheering for my team. I wasn't even thinking about my team. I was thinking about the real, live, and very scary buzzing bees behind me.

I ran away from them as fast as I could.

Yikes! Something big hit my foot. Was it a huge swarm of bees, about to give me horrible stings? Or was it one gigantic bee, about to give me the world's largest bee sting? Or was it a huge swarm of gigantic bees, about to give me thousands of the world's largest bee stings?

I looked down. There were no bees by my foot. The only thing by my foot was a soccer ball.

I dribbled the ball and kept running, dodging around the Red Hot Lightning players.

All around me, people cheered.

I got close to the goal.

I checked this time to make sure it wasn't my team's goal.

It was the Red Hot Lightning's goal.

I kicked the ball toward it.

The Red Hot Lightning's goalie dived for the ball.

He missed.

The ball went into the goal.

"Yahoo!" I shouted.

My teammates and their families and my family cheered.

"Nice shot, Zeke!" Hector called out.

"Good job," Rudy said.

"You got lucky," Owen grumbled.

I looked around. I had gotten very lucky. Bees were no longer chasing me. The only buzzing bees in sight were my Buzzing Bees teammates. They patted me on the back and gave me high fives.

Bolt said, "That almost makes up for your moronic goal for the other team last week."

My team was ahead by two points. The game was going great so far.

What could possibly go wrong?

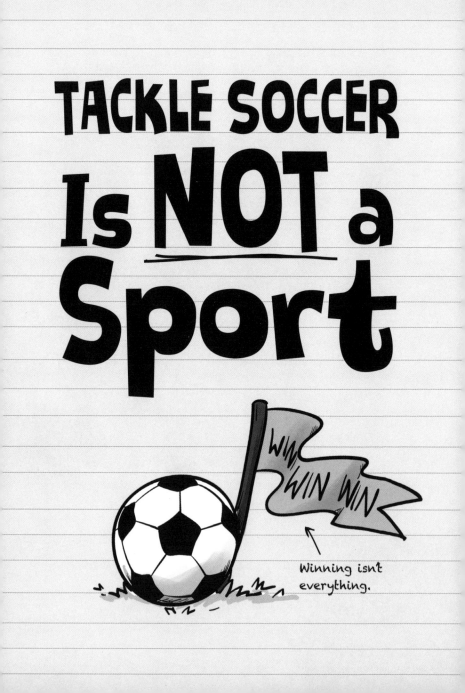

"We're ahead by two points. We'll win this game for sure," Bolt said.

"Win, win, win!" Bolt's mother chanted.

Hector got the ball for the Red Hot Lightning team. He ran quickly with it and dribbled it close to our goal.

"We have to win. Win, win, win," Bolt said. He raced toward Hector and didn't slow down when he got close.

"Slow down, Bolt!" I yelled. "This isn't tackle football! Soccer is a noncontact sport!" Noncontact meant that we weren't allowed to touch other players. We definitely weren't allowed to run into them at full speed.

But Bolt kept rushing toward Hector. He plowed into him and knocked him down.

The referee blew his whistle. "Foul by the Buzzing Bees," he said.

I hurried over to Hector and asked, "Are you okay?"

"My leg is scraped up and my arm is sore." Hector slowly stood and then pointed at Bolt. "You should watch where you're going."

"I was watching. I was watching you dribble the ball near our goal. I didn't want you to score a point, so I knocked you down," he said.

"Knocking people down on purpose is really mean. And it could get you kicked out of the game," I said.

"Mind your own business, Zeke," Bolt said.

"My best friend's safety *is* my business," I said.

The referee gave a warning to Bolt and a free kick to Hector.

Hector kicked the ball into the goal.

I cheered for him.

Bolt glared at me. "You shouldn't root for the other team."

"I'll root for my friend if I want to," I said.

A few minutes later, Bolt got the ball and dribbled it down the field.

I heard terrible sounds near Bolt. They were loud, screechy, and annoying. Unfortunately, I knew those sounds very well. They came from my little sister.

Mia was jumping rope and singing a Princess Sing-Along song in her screechy voice: "People who are very wise, la la la, make sure they get exercise, la la la. They run and swim and touch their toes, la la la. They don't just sit and pick their nose, la la la."

Mia didn't pay attention to where she was
going. She screeched the song and jumped rope
and screeched and jumped and screeched and
jumped — right onto the soccer field.

Bolt kept dribbling the ball down the field.
He got closer and closer to Mia. He was a lot
bigger than her. He was running very fast. He
could really hurt her. He could even kill her.

I yelled, "Bolt, watch out for my sister!"

Bolt yelled, "No! She should watch out for me! She shouldn't be on the soccer field!"

Just as Bolt was about to run into Mia, I grabbed him from behind and tackled him to the ground.

Bolt said with a sneer, "You told me before we weren't playing tackle football."

The referee blew his whistle.

Mom ran over and said, "Sorry my daughter got in the way. I should have been watching her more closely."

"You should never have let your annoying brat on the field," Bolt's mother said.

"You should never have let *your* annoying brat on the field," my mother replied.

"He's supposed to be on the field. He's on the team," Bolt's mother said.

"I wish he weren't on the team. He's an annoying brat," Mom said.

The referee blew his whistle again. He said, "Stop arguing."

"Sorry," Mom said again.

"And I'm sorry for accidentally getting on the field," Mia said.

"I'm not sorry at all," Bolt's mother said.

My mom and sister returned to their seats on the sideline.

The referee gave Bolt another warning. He gave the ball to the Red Hot Lightning.

"That's no fair. I should get the ball," Bolt said. He punched and kicked the air.

"You're an awful referee," Bolt's mother said. She punched and kicked the air too.

"You two are very poor sports. I'm kicking you both out of the game," the referee said.

Bolt shouted a bad word.

Bolt's mom shouted more bad words.

"Both of you get out of here *now*," Coach Hall said.

Bolt and his mother stomped off the field.

I felt like cheering.

Then I remembered that Bolt was the best player on our team. Without him, we would lose badly to my friends.

I no longer felt like cheering.

MY TEAM WINS . . .
the
SNACK CONTEST

At least we win at something.
Something delicious!

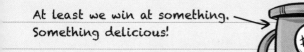

9

Once Bolt and his mother left the game, the Red Hot Lightning team quickly scored another goal.

My team got the ball. But we weren't sure what to do with it. Bolt had always taken the ball and shouted orders at us.

Luckily, Coach Hall helped us. He said, "Zeke, kick the ball to Tom."

So I passed the ball to Tom. He dribbled it a few feet.

Then a boy from Red Hot Lightning stole the ball. He passed it to one of his teammates, who kicked it into our goal.

I knew we'd lose the game without Bolt. He was a jerk, but he was also a good soccer player.

One of my teammates dribbled the ball a couple of yards and passed it to Raj.

A boy from Red Hot Lightning got the ball from Raj.

"Sorry," Raj said.

"Don't worry about it," I replied.

Then one of our teammates stole the ball from Red Hot Lightning. He dribbled it and passed it to me.

I tried to shoot the ball into the goal.

I missed.

I was glad that Bolt and his mother were gone. They would have yelled at me. Still, I felt bad about missing the goal.

Raj said, "Good try, Zeke."

I felt a little better.

Another boy said, "That was so close, Zeke."

I felt better.

Mia yelled, "Go, Buzzing Bees!"

I felt even better.

Mom yelled, "Hooray, Zekey! Go, sweetie, go!"

I felt embarrassed.

Red Hot Lightning soon got another goal. But I still enjoyed the game. Now that loud Bolt and his loud mother were gone, we could hear Coach Hall on the sideline. He gave us good tips about who to guard and who was open for passes. And without Bolt hogging the ball, everyone else on our team got more playing time.

We scored two more goals during the game. Unfortunately, Red Hot Lightning scored a lot more than that. They scored five or six or seven more goals. I didn't keep close count of the score. I had been too busy running for the ball, listening to Coach Hall's advice, and cheering for my teammates.

After the game, we all told the Red Hot Lightning Team, "Good game." I really meant it. Once Bolt and his mother left, it had become a good game.

I had thought losing to my friends would be embarrassing. But it wasn't. The only embarrassing thing was being on the same team as Bolt the annoying brat.

Tom's mother walked up to me as I rested on the field. She pointed to a large bag in her hands and said, "I brought snacks today. I made white chocolate cookies, chocolate chip cookies, sugar cookies, gingerbread cookies, and cinnamon raisin cookies. Each one is very sweet and very huge."

I licked my lips. All the cookies sounded delicious. I couldn't decide which one to choose.

Tom's mother handed me the bag. She said, "There's one of each kind of cookie in here. I hope you like them."

"They're all for me?" I asked.

She smiled. "Of course. I also brought chocolate milk, fruit punch, and lemonade. They're in the cooler. Help yourself."

"Thanks a lot. I love soccer!" I said.

Raj walked over to me. He held a bag of cookies in one hand and cartons of chocolate milk and lemonade in the other. He said, "Snacks are the best part of soccer."

I nodded. "We got fewer goals than Red Hot Lightning, but we got the most yummy snacks. Snacks are much more important than scores."

"Cookies are my second most favorite things in the world. Video games are my first most favorite things in the world," Raj said.

I smiled. "Video games are my first most favorite things in the world too."

"Do you have *Destroy and Demolish*?" Raj asked. "I'm stuck on the third level of that game."

"I was stuck on that one too. It took me a long time to figure out how to get to the next level," I said. "I can help you with it if you want."

"Can you come over tomorrow?" Raj asked.

"I'll ask my mom," I said.

I walked over to her and asked.

Mom patted my head. "*Aww.* You made a new friend. That's sweet."

I rolled my eyes.

"Speaking of sweet things, can I have a cookie?" Mia pointed to my big bag of cookies.

I shook my head. "The snack is for Buzzing Bees. It's not for the sisters of Buzzing Bees."

"You're selfish," Mia said.

"I'm not selfish. I saved your life today."

"You didn't exactly save her life. You just stopped her from getting hurt," Mom said.

"Mia didn't even thank me," I said.

"Thank you, Zeke. Can I have a cookie now?" Mia asked.

I shook my head again.

"But you have an entire bag of big cookies," she said.

"I played soccer for an entire hour, so I deserve an entire bag of big cookies," I said.

"Princess Sing-Along says junk food is bad for you." Mia screechily sang: "Tofu, spinach, beans, and seeds, la la la, are foods that your body needs, la la la. Foods with lots of chemicals, la la la, are extremely terrible, la la la."

"That song is extremely terrible," I said.

"Maybe you'll like this song better." Mia sang, "Junk food is a bad idea, la la la. It can give you diarrhe—"

I shoved a cookie into her mouth.

Mia started chewing and stopped singing. Giving up the cookie was worth it.

I returned to Raj and said, "After we play video games tomorrow, let's kick around a soccer ball."

"So we can try to win our next game?" Raj asked.

I shrugged.

SO WE CAN HAVE FUN.

Mom, Mia, and I walked into our house after my soccer game.

My older sister, Alexa, sat in the living room watching a TV movie. In the movie, a pretty woman was about to board a train. A handsome man ran toward the woman, calling out, "I love you, darling! I love you, darling! I love you, darling!"

I rolled my eyes and said, "We get it. He loves her. Does he have to keep repeating that? He's a pest. That woman should board the train and get away from him as fast as she can."

"Don't ruin my favorite movie. This scene is *soooo* romantic," Alexa said.

A commercial for aspirin came on.

"It's smart to advertise aspirin. This movie is giving me a headache," I said.

"*You* are giving me a headache," Alexa said.

"Be nice to Zeke. He saved me from getting hurt," Mia said.

"I saved your life," I said.

Alexa raised her eyebrows. "Huh? You saved her life?"

"Mia wandered onto the soccer field during the game. Zeke stopped a big jerk from running into her," Mom said.

Alexa shrugged. "Zeke, it sounds like you saved Mia from getting hurt. You didn't save her life. How did the soccer game go?"

"It was good," I said. "The big jerk on my team and his jerky mom got kicked out of the game. I cheered for my friends on the other team. I made a friend who loves video games. And I got a big bag of cookies."

"When I asked you about the soccer game, I just wanted to know the important thing: What was the score?" Alexa said.

"Oh. The score. The score was . . ." I tried to remember. My team got three or four goals. Red Hot Lightning scored seven or eight goals. I told Alexa, "I don't know the exact score."

"Zeke's team lost by a lot. A whole lot. A huge amount. The score wasn't even close. The Buzzing Bees lost big," Mia said.

"You don't have to rub it in, Mia. You should be nice to me. I saved your life," I said.

Mia shook her head. "You stopped me from getting hurt."

"*Shh.* My favorite movie is back on." Alexa pointed to the TV screen.

The handsome man ran up to the pretty woman, held her hand, and said, "Oh, my sweetheart."

At least he didn't say "I love you, darling" again.

Then he said, "I love you, darling. I love you, darling. I love you, darling."

Gross. I kind of hoped he'd fall onto the train tracks.

I picked up the remote control and changed channels. Oh, good. The sports station was showing a soccer game.

"Give me the remote," Alexa said.

I ignored her and stared at the TV.

"Mom, I'm trying to watch my favorite movie. Tell Zeke to give me back the remote control," Alexa said.

"You've seen that movie many times. You know how it ends. The pretty woman tells the handsome man she loves him. Then they kiss," Mom said.

I made a face. "*Eww.*"

"It's not *eww*. It's *aww*. It's *soooo* romantic," Alexa said.

I pretended to throw up.

"Is Princess Sing-Along in the movie?" Mia asked.

"No," Mom said.

"Are any other singing princesses in the movie?" Mia asked.

"No," Mom said.

"Are there any princesses at all in the movie?" Mia asked.

Mom shook her head.

"Then I don't want to see it," Mia said.

"Me neither," I said.

"I want to see it," Alexa said.

"Let Zeke have a turn with the TV. While you spent the morning watching TV, Zeke played a tough game of soccer and protected Mia from a mean boy," Mom said.

I nodded. "I may have saved Mia's life."

"You just stopped her from getting hurt," Mom said. "But you still deserve a turn to watch TV."

Alexa frowned and got off the couch.

Then she looked at the soccer game on TV.

She kept looking at it.

She returned to the couch and said, "Whoa. Those soccer players are *sooo* cute."

I pointed to the TV screen. "They're great at passing the ball to each other. It's important to work well as a team."

"Most importantly, they're gorgeous," Alexa said.

I rolled my eyes. "Gorgeous, shmorgeous. Who cares about that?"

"I do," Alexa said.

A commercial came on for diaper rash ointment. The woman on screen said:

Yuck. I didn't care how smooth and soft it was. I would never kiss anyone's bottom.

I changed the channel and saw a commercial for pimple cream. A huge red pimple covered the TV screen. White pus oozed out of it. Totally Gross.

Mia sang, "Wash your face every day, la la la, to keep the pimples away, la la la."

I changed the channel again. Alexa's favorite movie was still on. The handsome actor and the pretty actress were kissing. Yuck.

I gave Alexa the remote control. Then I asked Mom if I could go outside.

"What for?" Mom asked.

"To see if the kids in the neighborhood want to kick around a soccer ball."

"Good idea. If you practice a lot, your soccer skills will get better and better. You and your team might win some games," Mom said.

My mom was smart about some things but not about soccer.

I explained to her, "I mostly want to have fun, get some exercise, and make friends. There's a lot more to soccer than just trying to win games."

Then I ran outside.

ABOUT THE AUTHOR

D. L. Green lives in California with her husband, three children, silly dog, and a big collection of rubber chickens. She loves to read, write, and joke around.

ABOUT THE ILLUSTRATOR

Josh Alves has never scored a goal. He has also never played soccer. Josh loves drawing in his studio (a.k.a. "Drawing Closet") in Maine, where he lives with his wonderful wife and their four kids!

HAVE YOU EVER DONE SOMETHING AS STUPID AS SCORING A GOAL FOR THE OTHER TEAM?

(And other really important questions)

Write answers to these questions, or discuss them with your friends and classmates.

1. Have you ever done something as stupid as scoring a goal for the other team? What was it? How did you recover from the embarrassment?

2. Clearly, the Buzzing Bees is a terrible name for a soccer team. What would you name a team with urine-colored uniforms?

3. I tried to get out of playing soccer against my friends' team, but my mom wouldn't let me. Can you think of a way I could have gotten out of it?

4. By the way, why was it so important to my mom that I went to the game, anyway?

5. What is the best thing about being in a sport or activity? (And it is okay if you say the snack . . .)

BIG WORDS
according to Zeke

TRY USING THEM IN SENTENCES JUST LIKE I DO

<u>ACCIDENTALLY</u>: When you do something bad by mistake or without even thinking about it.

<u>ADVERTISE</u>: Using commercials and ads to get people to buy or like things.

<u>ALLERGIC</u>: When you are allergic to something, being around it makes you sick. I think I'm allergic to Princess Sing-Along.

<u>ANNOYING</u>: Things that are annoying bug you so much you think you might lose it!

<u>ATTITUDE</u>: Your attitude is how you think and act. I have a great attitude about video games. I have a bad attitude about homework.

<u>COMMERCIAL</u>: A short, often boring thing on television. Commercials break into your shows and try to sell you things.

<u>CONCLUSION</u>: A final decision. After thinking about all the facts, my conclusion was that soccer was lame.

<u>DEFENSE</u>: The team that does NOT have the ball. Our team played defense a lot.

DEFINITELY: For sure!

DISTRACTED: If you get distracted, you can't remember what you were thinking or talking about. I love to distract Mr. McNutty.

EMBARRASSING: Something that's embarrassing makes you want to hide in your room. Under the covers. Or maybe the bed.

EXTREMELY: Super-duper, very much so.

GORGEOUS: I guess it means good looking or pretty. But, seriously, who cares?

INSULT: Something said that makes someone else feel sad or mad.

INTERRUPTIONS: Talking or actions that cut-off someone when he or she is talking. Grown-ups don't like interruptions.

MORON: A really dumb person, like someone who scores for the wrong team.

PENALTY: A punishment given in a game for breaking rules.

SCREECHY: Loud and high-pitched and awful! In other words, everything that has to do with Princess Sing-Along.

TERRORIZE: To scare and fill with complete fear. Grace Chang is an expert at terrorizing. So are fleas.

Bees also terrorize.

Score Some Fun!

If you're like me and want to have lots of fun when you're practicing soccer, give these games a try. Will they make you a soccer star? Maybe. Does it matter? Nope!

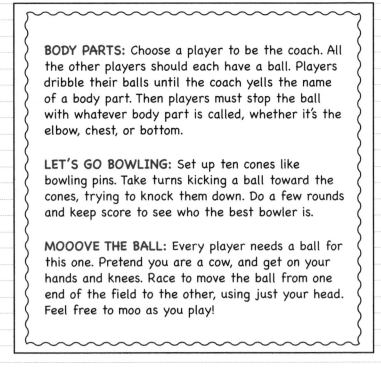

BODY PARTS: Choose a player to be the coach. All the other players should each have a ball. Players dribble their balls until the coach yells the name of a body part. Then players must stop the ball with whatever body part is called, whether it's the elbow, chest, or bottom.

LET'S GO BOWLING: Set up ten cones like bowling pins. Take turns kicking a ball toward the cones, trying to knock them down. Do a few rounds and keep score to see who the best bowler is.

MOOOVE THE BALL: Every player needs a ball for this one. Pretend you are a cow, and get on your hands and knees. Race to move the ball from one end of the field to the other, using just your head. Feel free to moo as you play!

GET CRABBY: Choose a few players to be the crabs, who crawl around on their hands and feet. The other players each dribble a ball, trying to avoid the crabs. If a crab catches a player, he or she must become a crab too.

STAY OUT OF MY YARD: Using cones, create a fence that splits the field in two. Next, divide players into two teams and give each player a ball. Set the timer for one minute. On go, players kick their balls over the fence into the other "yard." At the end of the minute, whoever has the least amount of balls on their side wins.

SHARKS AND MINNOWS: One player is the shark, while the rest of the players are the minnows. The shark stands in the middle of the field. The minnows line up at one end of the field, each with a ball. The minnows then try to dribble to the other end of the field, without the shark stealing away their ball. If you are caught, you are the new shark.

There are a lot of fun games to play with a soccer ball! →

AWESOME HAIR

CHARMING SMILE

COOLEST THIRD GRADER YOU'LL EVER MEET!

WWW.CAPSTONEKIDS.COM